The Jelly-Bean

by

F. Scott Fitzgerald

Rise of Douai

ISBN-13: 978-1495334061

ISBN-10: 1495334066

Introduction

In United States slang in the 1910s and early 1920s a "Jellybean" or "Jelly-Bean" was a young man who dressed stylishly to attract women but had little else to recommend him; similar to the older terms dandy and fop and the slightly later drugstore cowboy. F. Scott Fitzgerald wrote a story about such a character, The Jelly-Bean in 1920. Originally published in the periodical The Metropolitan, this story was first published in book form in Tales of the Jazz Age in 1922.

Francis Scott Key Fitzgerald (September 24, 1896 – December 21, 1940) was an American author of novels and short stories, whose works are the paradigmatic writings of the Jazz Age, a term he coined. He is widely regarded as one of the greatest American writers of the 20th century. Fitzgerald is considered a member of the "Lost Generation" of the 1920s. He finished four novels: This Side of Paradise, The Beautiful and Damned, The Great Gatsby (his most famous), and Tender Is the Night. A fifth, unfinished novel, The Love of the Last Tycoon, was published posthumously. Fitzgerald also wrote many short stories that treat themes of youth and promise along with age and despair.

Fitzgerald's work has inspired writers ever since he was first published. The publication of The Great Gatsby prompted T. S. Eliot to write, in a letter to Fitzgerald, "[I]t seems to me to be the first step that American fiction has taken since Henry James ...". Don Birnam, the protagonist of Charles Jackson's The Lost Weekend, says to himself, referring to The Great Gatsby, "There's no such thing ... as a flawless novel. But if there is, this is it." In letters written in the 1940s, J. D. Salinger expressed admiration of Fitzgerald's work, and his biographer Ian Hamilton wrote that Salinger even saw himself for some time as "Fitzgerald's successor." Richard Yates, a writer often compared to Fitzgerald, called The Great Gatsby "the most nourishing novel [he] read ... a miracle of talent ... a triumph of technique." It was written in a New York Times editorial after his death that Fitzgerald "was better than he knew, for in fact and in the literary sense he invented a generation ... He might have interpreted them and even guided them, as in their middle years they saw a different and nobler freedom threatened with destruction."

The Jelly-Bean

I

Jim Powell was a Jelly-bean. Much as I desire to make him an appealing character, I feel that it would be unscrupulous to deceive you on that point. He was a bred-in-the-bone, dyed-in-the-wool, ninety-nine three-quarters per cent Jelly-bean and he grew lazily all during Jelly-bean season, which is every season, down in the land of the Jelly-beans well below the Mason-Dixon line.

Now if you call a Memphis man a Jelly-bean he will quite possibly pull a long sinewy rope from his hip pocket and hang you to a convenient telegraph-pole. If you Call a New Orleans man a Jelly-bean he will probably grin and ask you who is taking your girl to the Mardi Gras ball. The particular Jelly-bean patch which produced the protagonist of this history lies somewhere between the two—a little city of forty thousand that has dozed sleepily for forty thousand years in southern Georgia occasionally stirring in its slumbers and muttering something about a war that took place sometime, somewhere, and that everyone else has forgotten long ago.

Jim was a Jelly-bean. I write that again because it has such a pleasant sound—rather like the beginning of a fairy story—as if Jim were nice. It somehow gives me a picture of him with a round, appetizing face and all sort of leaves and vegetables growing out of his cap. But Jim was long and thin and bent at the waist from stooping over pool-tables, and he was what might have been known in the indiscriminating North as a corner loafer. "Jelly-bean" is the name throughout the undissolved Confederacy for one who spends his life conjugating the verb to idle in the first person singular—I am idling, I have idled, I will idle.

Jim was born in a white house on a green corner, It had four weather-beaten pillars in front and a great amount of lattice-work in the rear that made a cheerful criss-cross background for a flowery sun-drenched lawn. Originally the dwellers in the white house had owned the ground next door and next door to that and next door to that, but this had been so long ago that even Jim's father, scarcely remembered it. He had, in fact, thought it a matter of so little moment that when he was dying from a pistol wound got in a brawl he neglected even to tell little Jim, who was five years old and miserably frightened. The white house became a boarding-house run by a tight-lipped lady from Macon, whom Jim called Aunt Mamie and detested with all his soul.

He became fifteen, went to high school, wore his hair in black snarls, and was afraid of girls. He hated his home where four women and one old man prolonged an interminable chatter from summer to summer about what lots the Powell place had originally included and what sorts of flowers would be out next. Sometimes the parents of little girls in town, remembering Jim's. mother and fancying a resemblance in the dark eyes and hair, invited him to parties, but parties made him shy and he much preferred sitting on a disconnected axle in Tilly's Garage, rolling the bones or exploring his mouth endlessly with a long straw. For pocket money, he picked up odd jobs, and it was due to this that he stopped going to parties. At his third party little

Marjorie Haight had whispered indiscreetly and within hearing distance that he was a boy who brought the groceries sometimes. So instead of the two-step and polka, Jim had learned to throw, any number he desired on the dice and had listened to spicy tales of all the shootings that had occurred in the surrounding country during the past fifty years.

He became eighteen. The war broke out and he enlisted as a gob and polished brass in the Charleston Navy-yard for a year. Then, by way of variety, he went North and polished brass in the Brooklyn Navy-yard for a year.

When the war was over he came home, He was twenty-one, has trousers were too short and too tight. His buttoned shoes were long and narrow. His tie was an alarming conspiracy of purple and pink marvellously scrolled, and over it were two blue eyes faded like a piece of very good old cloth, long exposed to the sun.

In the twilight of one April evening when a soft gray had drifted down along the cottonfields and over the sultry town, he was a vague figure leaning against a board fence, whistling and gazing at the moon's rim above the lights of Jackson Street. His mind was working persistently on a problem that had held his attention for an. The Jelly-bean had been invited to a party.

Back in the days when all the boys had detested all the girls, Clark Darrow and Jim had sat side by side in school. But, while Jim's social aspirations had died in the oily air of the garage, Clark had alternately fallen in and out of love, gone to college, taken to drink, given it up, and, in short, become one of the best beaux of the town. Nevertheless Clark and Jim had retained a friendship that, though casual, was perfectly definite. That afternoon Clark's ancient Ford had slowed up beside Jim, who was on the sidewalk and, out of a clear sky, Clark invited him to a party at the country club. The impulse that made him do this was no stranger than the impulse which made Jim accept. The latter was probably an unconscious ennui, a half-frightened sense of adventure. And now Jim was soberly thinking it over.

He began to sing, drumming his long foot idly on a stone block in the sidewalk till it wobbled up and down in time to the low throaty tune:

"One smile from Home in Jelly-bean town,
Lives Jeanne, the Jelly-bean Queen.
She loves her dice and treats 'em nice;
No dice would treat her mean."

He broke off and agitated the sidewalk to a bumpy gallop.

"Daggone!" he muttered, half aloud. They would all be there—the old crowd, the crowd to which, by right of the white house, sold long since, and the portrait of the officer in gray over the mantel, Jim should have belonged. But that crowd had grown up together into a tight little set as gradually as the girls' dresses had lengthened inch by inch, as definitely as the boys' trousers had dropped suddenly to their ankles. And to that society of first names and dead puppy loves Jim was an outsider—a running mate of poor whites. Most of the men knew him, condescendingly; he tipped his hat to three or four girls. That was all.

When the dusk had thickened into a blue setting for the moon, he walked through the hot, pleasantly pungent town to Jackson Street. The stores were closing and the last shoppers were drifting homeward, as if borne on the dreamy revolution of a slow merry-go-round. A street-fair farther down a brilliant alley of varicolored booths and contributed a blend of music to the night—an oriental dance on a calliope, a melancholy bugle in front of a freak show, a cheerful rendition of "Back Home in Tennessee" on a hand-organ.

The Jelly-bean stopped in a store and bought a collar. Then he sauntered along toward Soda Sam's, where he found the usual three or four cars of a summer evening parked in front and the little darkies running back and forth with sundaes and lemonades.

"Hello, Jim."

It was a voice at his elbow—Joe Ewing sitting in an automobile with Marylyn Wade. Nancy Lamar and a strange man were in the back seat.

The Jelly-bean tipped his hat quickly.

"Hi Ben—" then, after an almost imperceptible pause—"How y' all?"

Passing, he ambled on toward the garage where he had a room up-stairs. His "How y'all" had been said to Nancy Lamar, to whom he had not spoken in fifteen years.

Nancy had a mouth like a remembered kiss and shadowy eyes and blue-black hair inherited from her mother who had been born in Budapest. Jim passed her often on the street, walking small-boy fashion with her hands in her pockets and he knew that with her inseparable Sally Carrol Hopper she had left a trail of broken hearts from Atlanta to New Orleans.

For a few fleeting moments Jim wished he could dance. Then he laughed and as he reached his door began to sing softly to himself:

"Her Jelly Roll can twist your soul,
Her eyes are big and brown,
She's the Queen of the Queens of the Jelly-beans—
My Jeanne of Jelly-bean Town."

II

At nine-thirty, Jim and Clark met in front of Soda Sam's and started for the Country Club in Clark's Ford. "Jim," asked Clark casually, as they rattled through the jasmine-scented night, "how do you keep alive?"

The Jelly-bean paused, considered.

"Well," he said finally, "I got a room over Tilly's garage. I help him some with the cars in the afternoon an' he gives it to me free. Sometimes I drive one of his taxies and pick up a little thataway. I get fed up doin' that regular though."

"That all?"

"Well, when there's a lot of work I help him by the day—Saturdays usually—and then there's one main source of revenue I don't generally mention. Maybe you don't recollect I'm about the champion crap-shooter of this town. They make me shoot from a cup now because once I get the feel of a pair of dice they just roll for me."

Clark grinned appreciatively,

"I never could learn to set 'em so's they'd do what I wanted. Wish you'd shoot with Nancy Lamar some day and take all her money away from her. She will roll 'em with the boys and she loses more than her daddy can afford to give her. I happen to know she sold a good ring last month to pay a debt."

The Jelly-bean was noncommittal.

"The white house on Elm Street still belong to you?"

Jim shook his head.

"Sold. Got a pretty good price, seein' it wasn't in a good part of town no more. Lawyer told me to put it into Liberty bonds. But Aunt Mamie got so she didn't have no sense, so it takes all the interest to keep her up at Great Farms Sanitarium.

"Hm."

"I got an old uncle up-state an' I reckin I kin go up there if ever I get sure enough pore. Nice farm, but not enough niggers around to work it. He's asked me to come up and help him, but I don't guess I'd take much to it. Too doggone lonesome—" He broke off suddenly. "Clark, I want to tell you I'm much obliged to you for askin' me out, but I'd be a lot happier if you'd just stop the car right here an' let me walk back into town."

"Shucks!" Clark grunted. "Do you good to step out. You don't have to dance—just get out there on the floor and shake."

"Hold on," exclaimed. Jim uneasily, "Don't you go leadin' me up to any girls and leavin' me there so I'll have to dance with 'em."

Clark laughed.

"'Cause," continued Jim desperately, "without you swear you won't do that I'm agoin' to get out right here an' my good legs goin' carry me back to Jackson street."

They agreed after some argument that Jim, unmolested by females, was to view the spectacle from a secluded settee in the corner where Clark would join him whenever he wasn't dancing.

So ten o'clock found the Jelly-bean with his legs crossed and his arms conservatively folded, trying to look casually at home and politely uninterested in the dancers. At heart he was torn between overwhelming self-consciousness and an intense curiosity as to all that went on around him. He saw the girls emerge one by one from the dressing-room, stretching and pluming themselves like bright birds, smiling over their powdered shoulders at the chaperones, casting a quick glance around to take in the room and, simultaneously, the room's reaction to their entrance—and then, again like birds, alighting and nestling in the sober arms of their waiting escorts. Sally Carrol Hopper, blonde and lazy-eyed, appeared clad in her favorite pink and blinking like an awakened rose. Marjorie Haight, Marylyn Wade, Harriet Cary, all the girls he had seen loitering down Jackson Street by noon, now, curled and brilliantined and delicately tinted for the overhead lights, were miraculously strange Dresden figures of pink and blue and red and gold, fresh from the shop and not yet fully dried.

He had been there half an hour, totally uncheered by Clark's jovial visits which were each one accompanied by a "Hello, old boy, how you making out?" and a slap at his knee. A dozen males had spoken to him or stopped for a moment beside him, but he knew that they were each one surprised at finding him there and fancied that one or two were even slightly resentful. But at half past ten his embarrassment suddenly left him and a pull of breathless interest took him completely out of himself—Nancy Lamar had come out of the dressing-room.

She was dressed in yellow organdie, a costume of a hundred cool corners, with three tiers of ruffles and a big bow in back until she shed black and yellow around her in a sort of phosphorescent lustre. The Jelly-bean's eyes opened wide and a lump arose in his throat. For she stood beside the door until her partner hurried up. Jim recognized him as the stranger who had been with her in Joe Ewing's car that afternoon. He saw her set her arms akimbo and say something in a low voice, and laugh. The man laughed too and Jim experienced the quick pang of a weird new kind of pain. Some ray had passed between the pair, a shaft of beauty from that sun that had warmed him a moment since. The Jelly-bean felt suddenly like a weed in a shadow.

A minute later Clark approached him, bright-eyed and glowing.

" Hi, old man" he cried with some lack of originality. "How you making out?"

Jim replied that he was making out as well as could be expected.

"You come along with me," commanded Clark.

"I've got something that'll put an edge on the evening."

Jim followed him awkwardly across the floor and up the stairs to the locker-room where Clark produced a flask of nameless yellow liquid.

"Good old corn."

Ginger ale arrived on a tray. Such potent nectar as "good old corn" needed some disguise beyond seltzer.

"Say, boy," exclaimed Clark breathlessly, "doesn't Nancy Lamar look beautiful?"

Jim nodded.

"Mighty beautiful," he agreed.

"She's all dolled up to a fare-you-well to-night," continued Clark. "Notice that fellow she's with?"

"Big fella? White pants?"

"Yeah. Well, that's Ogden Merritt from Savannah. Old man Merritt makes the Merritt safety razors. This fella's crazy about her. Been chasing, after her all year.

"She's a wild baby," continued Clark, "but I like her. So does everybody. But she sure does do crazy stunts. She usually gets out alive, but she's got scars all over her reputation from one thing or another she's done."

"That so?" Jim passed over his glass. "That's good corn."

"Not so bad. Oh, she's a wild one. Shoot craps, say, boy! And she do like her high-balls. Promised I'd give her one later on."

"She in love with this—Merritt?"

" Damned if I know. Seems like all the best girls around here marry fellas and go off somewhere."

He poured himself one more drink and carefully corked the bottle.

"Listen, Jim, I got to go dance and I'd be much obliged if you just stick this corn right on your hip as long as you're not dancing. If a man notices I've had a drink he'll come up and ask me and before I know it it's all gone and somebody else is having my good time."

So Nancy Lamar was going to marry. This toast of a town was to become the private property of an individual in white trousers—and all because white trousers' father had made a better razor than his neighbor. As they descended the stairs Jim found the idea inexplicably depressing. For the first time in his life he felt a vague and romantic yearning. A picture of her began to form in his imagination—Nancy walking boylike and debonnaire along the street, taking an orange as tithe from a worshipful fruit-dealer, charging a dope on a mythical account, at Soda Sam's, assembling a convoy of beaux and then driving off in triumphal state for an afternoon of splashing and singing.

The Jelly-bean walked out on the porch to a deserted corner, dark between the moon on the lawn and the single lighted door of the ballroom. There he found a chair and, lighting a cigarette, drifted into the thoughtless reverie that was his usual mood. Yet now it was a reverie made sensuous by the night and by the hot smell of damp powder puffs, tucked in the fronts of low dresses and distilling a thousand rich scents, to float out through the open door. The music itself, blurred by a loud trombone, became hot and shadowy, a languorous overtone to the scraping of many shoes and slippers.

Suddenly the square of yellow light that fell through the door was obscured by a dark figure. A girl had come out of the dressing-room and was standing on the porch not more than ten feet away. Jim heard a low-breathed "doggone" and then she turned and saw him. It was Nancy Lamar.

Jim rose to his feet.

"Howdy?"

"Hello—" she paused, hesitated and then approached. "Oh, it's—Jim Powell."

He bowed slightly, tried to think of a casual remark.

"Do you suppose," she began quickly, "I mean—do you know anything about gum?"

"What?" "I've got gum on my shoe. Some utter ass left his or her gum on the floor and of course I stepped in it."

Jim blushed, inappropriately.

"Do you know how to get it off?" she demanded petulantly. "I've tried a knife. I've tried every damn thing in the dressing-room. I've tried soap and water—and even perfume and I've ruined my powder-puff trying to make it stick to that."

Jim considered the question in some agitation.

"Why—I think maybe gasolene—"

The words had scarcely left his lips when she grasped his hand and pulled him at a run off the low veranda, over a flower bed and at a gallop toward a group of cars parked in the moonlight by the first hole of the golf course.

"Turn on the gasolene," she commanded breathlessly.

"What?"

"For the gum of course. I've got to get it off. I can't dance with gum on."

Obediently Jim turned to the cars and began inspecting them with a view to obtaining the desired solvent. Had she demanded a cylinder he would have done his best to wrench one out.

" Here," he said after a moment's search. "'Here's one that's easy. Got a handkerchief?"

"It's up-stairs wet. I used it for the soap and water."

Jim laboriously explored his pockets.

"Don't believe I got one either."

"Doggone it! Well, we can turn it on and let it run on the ground."

He turned the spout; a dripping began.

"More!"

He turned it on fuller. The dripping became a flow and formed an oily pool that glistened brightly, reflecting a dozen tremulous moons on its quivering bosom.

"Ah," she sighed contentedly, "let it all out. The only thing to do is to wade in it."

In desperation he turned on the tap full and the pool suddenly widened sending tiny rivers and trickles in all directions.

"That's fine. That's something like."

Raising her skirts she stepped gracefully in.

"I know this'll take it off," she murmured.

Jim smiled.

"There's lots more cars."

She stepped daintily out of the gasolene and began scraping her slippers, side and bottom, on the running-board of the automobile. The jelly-bean contained himself no longer. He bent double with explosive laughter and after a second she joined in.

"You're here with Clark Darrow, aren't you?" she asked as they walked back toward the veranda.

"Yes."

"You know where he is now?"

"Out dancin', I reckin."

"The deuce. He promised me a highball."

"Well," said Jim, "I guess that'll be all right. I got his bottle right here in my pocket."

She smiled at him radiantly.

"I guess maybe you'll need ginger ale though," he added.

"Not me. Just the bottle."

"Sure enough?"

She laughed scornfully.

"Try me. I can drink anything any man can. Let's sit down."

She perched herself on the side of a table and he dropped into one of the wicker chairs beside her. Taking out the cork she held the flask to her lips and took a long drink. He watched her fascinated.

"Like it?"

She shook her head breathlessly.

"No, but I like the way it makes me feel. I think most people are that way."

Jim agreed.

"My daddy liked it too well. It got him."

"American men," said Nancy gravely, "don't know how to drink."

"What?" Jim was startled.

"In fact," she went on carelessly, "they don't know

how to do anything very well. The one thing I regret in my life is that I wasn't born in England."

"In England?"

"Yes. It's the one regret of my life that I wasn't."

"Do you like it over there?" "Yes. Immensely. I've never been there in person, but I've met a lot of Englishmen who were over here in the army, Oxford and Cambridge men—you know, that's like Sewanee and University of Georgia are here—and of course I've read a lot of English novels."

Jim was interested, amazed.

"D' you ever hear of Lady Diana Manner?" she asked earnestly.

No, Jim had not.

"Well, she's what I'd like to be. Dark, you know, like me, and wild as sin. She's the girl who rode her horse up the steps of some cathedral or church or something and all the novelists made their heroines do it afterwards."

Jim nodded politely. He was out of his depths.

"Pass the bottle," suggested Nancy. "I'm going to take another little one. A little drink wouldn't hurt a baby.

"You see," she continued, again breathless after a draught. "People over there have style, Nobody has style here. I mean the boys here aren't really worth dressing up for or doing sensational things for. Don't you know?"

"I suppose so—I mean I suppose not," murmured Jim.

"And I'd like to do 'em an' all. I'm really the only girl in town that has style."

She stretched, out her arms and yawned pleasantly.

"Pretty evening."

"Sure is," agreed Jim.

"Like to have boat" she suggested dreamily. "Like to sail out on a silver lake, say the Thames, for instance. Have champagne and caviare sandwiches along. Have about eight people. And one of the men would jump overboard to amuse the party, and get drowned like a man did with Lady Diana Manners once."

"Did he do it to please her?" "Didn't mean drown himself to please her. He just meant to jump overboard and make everybody laugh,"

"I reckin they just died laughin' when he drowned."

"Oh, I suppose they laughed a little," she admitted. "I imagine she did, anyway. She's pretty hard, I guess—like I am."

" You hard?"

"Like nails." She yawned again and added, "Give me a little more from that bottle."

Jim hesitated but she held out her hand defiantly, "Don't treat me like a girl;" she warned him. "I'm not like any girl you ever saw," She considered. "Still, perhaps you're right. You got—you got old head on young shoulders."

She jumped to her feet and moved toward the door. The Jelly-bean rose also.

"Good-bye," she said politely, "good-bye. Thanks, Jelly-bean."

Then she stepped inside and left him wide-eyed upon the porch.

III

At twelve o'clock a procession of cloaks issued single file from the women's dressing-room and, each one pairing with a coated beau like dancers meeting in a cotillion figure, drifted through the door with sleepy happy laughter—through the door into the dark where autos backed and snorted and parties called to one another and gathered around the water-cooler.

Jim, sitting in his corner, rose to look for Clark. They had met at eleven; then Clark had gone in to dance. So, seeking him, Jim wandered into the soft-drink stand that had once been a bar. The room was deserted except for a sleepy negro dozing behind the counter and two boys lazily fingering a pair of dice at one of the tables. Jim was about to leave when he saw Clark coming in. At the same moment Clark looked up.

"Hi, Jim" he commanded. "C'mon over and help us with this bottle. I guess there's not much left, but there's one all around."

Nancy, the man from Savannah, Marylyn Wade, and Joe Ewing were lolling and laughing in the doorway. Nancy caught Jim's eye and winked at him humorously.

They drifted over to a table and arranging themselves around it waited for the waiter to bring ginger ale. Jim, faintly ill at ease, turned his eyes on Nancy, who had drifted into a nickel crap game with the two boys at the next table.

"Bring them over here," suggested Clark.

Joe looked around.

"We don't want to draw a crowd. It's against club rules.

"Nobody's around," insisted Clark, "except Mr. Taylor. He's walking up and down, like a wild-man trying find out who let all the gasolene out of his car."

There was a general laugh.

"I bet a million Nancy got something on her shoe again. You can't park when she's around."

"O Nancy, Mr. Taylor's looking for you!"

Nancy's cheeks were glowing with excitement over the game. "I haven't seen his silly little flivver in two weeks."

Jim felt a sudden silence. He turned and saw an individual of uncertain age standing in the doorway.

Clark's voice punctuated the embarrassment.

"Won't you join us Mr. Taylor?"

"Thanks."

Mr. Taylor spread his unwelcome presence over a chair. "Have to, I guess. I'm waiting till they dig me up some gasolene. Somebody got funny with my car."

His eyes narrowed and he looked quickly from one to the other. Jim wondered what he had heard from the doorway—tried to remember what had been said.

"I'm right to-night," Nancy sang out, "and my four bits is in the ring."

" Faded!" snapped Taylor suddenly.

"Why, Mr. Taylor, I didn't know you shot craps!" Nancy was overjoyed to find that he had seated himself and instantly covered her bet. They had openly disliked each other since the night she had definitely discouraged a series of rather pointed advances.

"All right, babies, do it for your mamma. Just one

little seven." Nancy was cooing to the dice. She rattled them with a brave underhand flourish, and rolled them out on the table.

"Ah-h! I suspected it. And now again with the dollar up."

Five passes to her credit found Taylor a bad loser. She was making it personal, and after each success Jim watched triumph flutter across her face. She was doubling with each throw—such luck could scarcely last. "Better go easy," he cautioned her timidly.

"Ah, but watch this one," she whispered. It was eight on the dice and she called her number.

"Little Ada, this time we're going South."

Ada from Decatur rolled over the table. Nancy was flushed and half-hysterical, but her luck was holding.

She drove the pot up and up, refusing to drag. Taylor was drumming with his fingers on the table but he was in to stay.

Then Nancy tried for a ten and lost the dice. Taylor seized them avidly. He shot in silence, and in the hush of excitement the clatter of one pass after another on the table was the only sound.

Now Nancy had the dice again, but her luck had broken. An hour passed. Back and forth it went. Taylor had been at it again—and again and again. They were even at last—Nancy lost her ultimate five dollars.

" Will you take my check," she said quickly, "for fifty, and we'll shoot it all?" Her voice was a little unsteady and her hand shook as she reached to the money.

Clark exchanged an uncertain but alarmed glance with Joe Ewing. Taylor shot again. He had Nancy's check.

"How 'bout another?" she said wildly. "Jes' any bank'll do—money everywhere as a matter of fact."

Jim understood—-the "good old corn" he had given her—the "good old corn" she had taken since. He wished he dared interfere—a girl of that age and position would hardly have two bank accounts. When the clock struck two he contained himself no longer.

"May I—can't you let me roll 'em for you?" he suggested, his low, lazy voice a little strained.

Suddenly sleepy and listless, Nancy flung the dice down before him.

"All right—old boy! As Lady Diana Manners says, 'Shoot 'em, Jelly-bean'—My luck's gone."

"Mr. Taylor," said Jim, carelessly, "we'll shoot for one of those there checks against the cash."

Half an hour later Nancy swayed forward and clapped him on the back.

"Stole my luck, you did." She was nodding her head sagely.

Jim swept up the last check and putting it with the others tore them into confetti and scattered them on the floor. Someone started singing and Nancy kicking her chair backward rose to her feet.

"Ladies and gentlemen," she announced, "Ladies—that's you Marylyn. I want to tell the world that Mr. Jim Powell, who is a well-known Jelly-bean of this city, is an exception to the great rule—'lucky in dice—unlucky in love.' He's lucky in dice, and as matter of fact I—I love him. Ladies and gentlemen, Nancy Lamar, famous dark-haired beauty often featured in the Herald as one the most popular members of younger set as other girls are often featured in this particular case; Wish to announce—wish to announce, anyway, Gentlemen—" She tipped suddenly. Clark caught her and restored her balance.

"My error," she laughed, "she—stoops to—stoops to—anyways—We'll drink to Jelly-bean ... Mr. Jim Powell, King of the Jelly-beans."

And a few minutes later as Jim waited hat in hand for Clark in the darkness of that same corner of the porch where she had come searching for gasolene, she appeared suddenly beside him.

"Jelly-bean," she said, "are you here, Jelly-bean? I think—" and her slight unsteadiness seemed part of an enchanted dream—"I think you deserve one of my sweetest kisses for that, Jelly-bean."

For an instant her arms were around his neck—her lips were pressed to his.

"I'm a wild part of the world, Jelly-bean, but you did me a good turn."

Then she was gone, down the porch, over the cricket-loud lawn. Jim saw Merritt come out the front door and say something to her angrily—saw her laugh and, turning away, walk with averted eyes to his car. Marylyn and Joe followed, singing a drowsy song about a Jazz baby.

Clark came out and joined Jim on the steps. "All pretty lit, I guess," he yawned. "Merritt's in a mean mood. He's certainly off Nancy."

Over east along the golf course a faint rug of gray spread itself across the feet of the night. The party in the car began to chant a chorus as the engine warmed up.

"Good-night everybody," called Clark.

" Good-night, Clark."

"Good-night."

There was a pause, and then a soft, happy voice added,

"Good-night, Jelly-bean."

The car drove off to a burst of singing. A rooster on a farm across the way took up a solitary mournful crow, and behind them, a last negro waiter turned out the porch light, Jim and Clark strolled over toward the Ford, their, shoes crunching raucously on the gravel drive.

"Oh boy!" sighed Clark softly, "how you can set those dice!"

It was still too dark for him to see the flush on Jim's thin cheeks—or to know that it was a flush of unfamiliar shame.

IV

Over Tilly's garage a bleak room echoed all day to the rumble and snorting down-stairs and the singing of the negro washers as they turned the hose on the cars outside. It was a cheerless square of a room, punctuated with a bed and a battered table on which lay half a dozen books—Joe Miller's "Slow Train thru Arkansas," "Lucille," in an old edition very much annotated in an old-fashioned hand; "The Eyes of the World," by Harold Bell Wright, and an ancient prayer-book of the Church of England with the name Alice Powell and the date 1831 written on the fly-leaf.

The East, gray when Jelly-bean entered the garage, became a rich and vivid blue as he turned on his solitary electric light. He snapped it out again, and going to the window rested his elbows on the sill and stared into the deepening morning. With the awakening of his emotions, his first perception was a sense of futility, a dull ache at the utter grayness of his life. A wall had sprung up suddenly around him hedging him in, a wall as definite and tangible as the white wall of his bare room. And with his perception of this wall all that had been the romance of his existence, the casualness, the light-hearted improvidence, the miraculous open-handedness of life faded out. The Jelly-bean strolling up Jackson Street humming a lazy song, known at every shop and street stand, cropful of easy greeting and local wit, sad sometimes for only the sake of sadness and the flight of time—that Jelly-bean was suddenly vanished. The very name was a reproach, a triviality. With a flood of insight he knew that Merritt must despise him, that even Nancy's kiss in the dawn would have awakened not jealousy but only a contempt for Nancy's so lowering herself. And on his part the Jelly-bean had used for her a dingy subterfuge learned from the garage. He had been her moral laundry; the stains were his.

As the gray became blue, brightened and filled the room, he crossed to his bed and threw himself down on it, gripping the edges fiercely.

"I love her," he cried aloud, "God!"

As he said this something gave way within him like a lump melting in his throat. The air cleared and became radiant with dawn, and turning over on his face he began to sob dully into the pillow.

In the sunshine of three o'clock Clark Darrow chugging painfully along Jackson Street was hailed by the Jelly-bean, who stood on the curb with his fingers in his vest pockets.

"Hi!" called Clark, bringing his Ford to an astonishing stop alongside. "Just get up?"

The Jelly-bean shook his head.

" Never did go to bed. Felt sorta restless, so I took a long walk this morning out in the country. Just got into town this minute."

"Should think you would feel restless. I been feeling thataway all day—"

"I'm thinkin' of leavin' town" continued the Jelly-bean, absorbed by his own thoughts. "Been thinkin' of goin' up on the farm, and takin' a little that work off Uncle Dun. Reckin I been bummin' too long."

Clark was silent and the Jelly-bean continued:

"I reckin maybe after Aunt Mamie dies I could sink that money of mine in the farm and make somethin' out of it. All my people originally came from that part up there. Had a big place."

Clark looked at him curiously.

"That's funny," he said. "This—this sort of affected me the same way."

The Jelly-bean hesitated.

"I don't know," he began slowly, "somethin' about—about that girl last night talkin' about a lady named Diana Manners—an English lady, sorta got me thinkin'!" He drew himself up and looked oddly at Clark, "I had a family once," he said defiantly.

Clark nodded.

"I know."

"And I'm the last of 'em," continued the Jelly-bean his voice rising slightly, "and I ain't worth shucks. Name they call me by means jelly—weak and wobbly like. People who weren't nothin' when my folks was a lot turn up their noses when they pass me on the street."

Again Clark was silent.

"So I'm through, I'm goin' to-day. And when I come back to this town it's going to be like a gentleman."

Clark took out his handkerchief and wiped his damp brow.

"Reckon you're not the only one it shook up," he admitted gloomily. "All this thing of girls going round like they do is going to stop right quick. Too bad, too, but everybody'll have to see it thataway."

"Do you mean," demanded Jim in surprise, "that all that's leaked out?"

"Leaked out? How on earth could they keep it secret. It'll be announced in the papers to-night. Doctor Lamar's got to save his name somehow."

Jim put his hands on the sides of the car and tightened his long fingers on the metal.

"Do you mean Taylor investigated those checks?"

It was Clark's turn to be surprised.

"Haven't you heard what happened?"

Jim's startled eyes were answer enough.

"Why," announced Clark dramatically, "those four got another bottle of corn, got tight and decided to shock the town—so Nancy and that fella Merritt were married in Rockville at seven o'clock this morning."

A tiny indentation appeared in the metal under the Jelly-bean's fingers.

"Married?"

"Sure enough. Nancy sobered up and rushed back into town, crying and frightened to death—claimed it'd all been a mistake. First Doctor Lamar went wild and was going to kill Merritt, but finally they got it patched up some way, and Nancy and Merritt went to Savannah on the two-thirty train."

Jim closed his eyes and with an effort overcame a sudden sickness.

"It's too bad," said Clark philosophically. "I don't mean the wedding—reckon that's all right, though I don't guess Nancy cared a darn about him. But it's a crime for a nice girl like that to hurt her family that way."

The Jelly-bean let go the car and turned away. Again something was going on inside him, some inexplicable but almost chemical change.

"Where you going?" asked Clark.

The Jelly-bean turned and looked dully back over his shoulder.

"Got to go," he muttered. "Been up too long; feelin' right sick."

"Oh."

The street was hot at three and hotter still at four, the April dust seeming to enmesh the sun and give it forth again as a world-old joke forever played on an eternity of afternoons. But at half past four a first layer of quiet fell and the shades lengthened under the awnings and heavy foliaged trees. In this heat nothing mattered. All life was weather, a waiting through the hot where events had no significance for the cool that was soft and caressing like a woman's hand on a tired forehead. Down in Georgia there is a feeling—perhaps inarticulate—that this is the greatest wisdom of the South—so after a while the Jelly-bean turned into a poolhall on Jackson Street where he was sure to find a congenial crowd who would make all the old jokes—the ones he knew.

THE END

- AN IDIOT'S GUIDE TO: BEE HUNTING BY JOHN LOCKARD, EDITED BY ARSALAN AHMED (2012)(PAPERBACK) ISBN-10: 1478383550

- THE RISE OF DOUAI BY ARSALAN AHMED (2012)(PAPERBACK) ISBN-10: 1479267783

- THE RICHEST MAN IN BABYLON BY GEORGE S. CLASON (2012) (PAPERBACK) ISBN-10: 1479377341

- THINK AND GROW RICH BY NAPOLEON HILL (2012) (PAPERBACK) ISBN-10: 1480061638

- AS A MAN THINKETH BY MR JAMES ALLEN (2012) (PAPERBACK) ISBN-10: 1480088161
- HOW TO ANALYZE PEOPLE ON

SIGHT BY ELSIE BENEDICT (PAPERBACK) ISBN-10: 1480081272

- THE ART OF WAR BY MR SUN TZU (PAPERBACK) ISBN-10: 1480082007
- MACBETH BY MR WILLIAM SHAKESPEARE (PAPERBACK) ISBN-10: 1480060682
- A CHRISTMAS CAROL BY MR CHARLES DICKENS ISBN-10: 1481194755
- CREATING CAPITAL: MONEY-MAKING AS AN AIM IN BUSINESS BY MR FREDRICK L LIPMAN ISBN-10: 1481158996
- GETTING GOLD: A PRACTICAL TREATISE FOR PROSPECTORS, MINERS, AND STUDENTS BY MR JOSEPH COLIN FRANCIS JOHNSON ISBN-10: 1481090984
- THE INTERPRETATION OF DREAMS BY MR SIGMUND FREUD ISBN-10: 1481134558
- THE COMMUNIST MANIFESTO BY MR KARL MARX AND MR FRIDRICK ENGLES ISBN-10:

1480112445

- THE PRINCE BY MR NICCOLO MACHIAVELLI ISBN-10: 1480119601
- THE WAY TO WEALTH BY MR BENJAMIN FRANKLIN ISBN-10: 1480099651
- THE ART OF MONEY GETTING - OR GOLDEN RULES FOR MAKING MONEY (SUCCESS PRINCIPLES) BY MR PHINEAS TAYLOR BARNUM ISBN-10: 1480138622

Twitter : **@RiseofDouai**

CPSIA information can be obtained
at www.ICGtesting.com
Printed in the USA
LVOW13s1748300917
550696LV00015B/2035/P